Never Talk to Strangers

ISBN-13: 978-0-545-20267-1
ISBN-10: 0-545-20267-1

Originally published in 1967 by Western Publishing Company, Inc.

12 11 10 9 8 7 6 5 12 13 14/0

Printed in the U.S.A. 40

First Scholastic printing, September 2009

Never Talk to Strangers

By Irma Joyce

Illustrated by George Buckett

SCHOLASTIC INC.
New York Toronto London Auckland Sydney
Mexico City New Delhi Hong Kong Buenos Aires

If you are hanging from a trapeze
And up sneaks a camel with bony knees,
Remember this rule, if you please—
Never talk to strangers.

If you are shopping in a store
And a spotted leopard leaps through the door,
Don't ask him what he's shopping for.
Never talk to strangers.

If the doorbell rings, and standing there
Is a grouchy, grumbling grizzly bear,
Shut the door. Your mother won't care.
Never talk to strangers.

If you are in the park for a walk
And out of a cloud parachutes a hawk,
Unless you know his name, don't talk.
Never talk to strangers.

If you are waiting for a bus
And behind you stands a rhinoceros,

Though he may shove and make a fuss,
Never talk to strangers.

If you are out for a mountain climb
And a coyote asks if you know the time,
Let him wait for a clock to chime.
Never talk to strangers.

If you're mailing a letter to Aunt Lucille
And you see a car with a whale at the wheel,
Stay away from him and his automobile.
Never talk to strangers.

If you are riding your bike at noon

And you see a bee with a bass bassoon,

Don't stop to ask the name of his tune.
Never talk to strangers.

If you are swimming in a pool
And a crocodile begins to drool,
Paddle away and repeat this rule—
Never talk to strangers.

But . . . if your father introduces you
To a roly-poly kangaroo,
Say politely, "How do you do?"
That's not talking to strangers,
Because your father knows her.

If your teacher says she'd like you to meet
A lilac llama who's very sweet,

Invite her over and serve a treat.
That's not talking to strangers,
Because your teacher knows her.

If a pal of yours you've always known
Brings around a prancing roan,
Welcome him in a friendly tone.

That's not talking to strangers,
Because your pal knows him.

If while eating toast and honey,
You catch a glimpse of the Easter Bunny,

Tell him a joke. He'll think it's funny.
That's not talking to strangers,
Because *everyone* knows him.

Now I'll tell you why you've never heard
This jolly giraffe say a single word.
It's because he learned from a little bird—
Never talk to strangers!

LION